Adam & Eve's FIRST SUNSET

GOD'S NEW DAY

SANDY EISENBERG SASSO

ILLUSTRATED BY JOANI KELLER ROTHENBERG

For People of All Faiths, All Backgrounds

JEWISH LIGHTS Publishing

Woodstock, Vermont

To Debbie, David and Dana—
and your promise of tomorrow

Mom (S.E.S.)

To Jeff,
you lighten my days
and embrace my nights

J.K.R.

Adam & Eve's First Sunset: God's New Day

2003 First Printing
Text © 2003 by Sandy Eisenberg Sasso
Illustrations © 2003 by Joani Keller Rothenberg

Library of Congress Cataloging-in-Publication Data
Sasso, Sandy Eisenberg.
Adam and Eve's first sunset : God's new day / by Sandy Eisenberg Sasso ; illustrated by Joani Keller Rothenberg.
        p. cm.
ISBN 1-58023-177-2 (hardcover)
1. Adam (Biblical figure)—Juvenile literature. 2. Eve (Biblical figure)—Juvenile literature. 3. Midrash—Juvenile literature. 4. Sun—Rising and setting—Juvenile literature. 5. Fear—Juvenile literature. 6. Gratitude—Juvenile literature. [1. Adam (Biblical figure) 2. Eve (Biblical figure) 3. Midrash. 4. Sun—Folklore.]
I. Rothenberg, Joani, 1964– ill. II. Title.
BS580.A4S38 2003
222'.1109505—dc21
                                                                                2003006830

10   9   8   7   6   5   4   3   2   1

Manufactured in Singapore
Book and jacket design: Bridgett Taylor

For People of All Faiths, All Backgrounds
Published by Jewish Lights Publishing
A Division of LongHill Partners, Inc.
Sunset Farm Offices, Route 4, P.O. Box 237
Woodstock, VT 05091
Tel (802) 457-4000   Fax (802) 457-4004
www.jewishlights.com

When the sun sank
at the termination of the Sabbath,
darkness began to set in.

Adam was terrified....What did God do for him?

God caused him to find two flints,
which he struck against each other.

Light came forth and Adam uttered a blessing over it.

—Genesis Rabbah 11:2

The sun was sinking beneath the clouds, falling behind the mountains, going down below the eagles' nests. The sky became darker, the air colder.

Perhaps the sun is tired,
thought Adam.

"You may rest on my
shoulders," he told the sun.

Perhaps the sun is just sad,
thought Eve.

"I will sing you a song,"
she said to the sun.

Adam was certain he could bring back the sun. Eve was sure she could convince the sun to return. But the sun sank lower in the sky. The light of day was waning.

Adam and Eve turned their faces to the sky and yelled at the sun. "God said we are the ones in charge. You must listen to us!"

But their words didn't matter. The sun kept sinking farther and farther in the sky.

Adam and Eve folded their arms across their chests. "It's your fault the sun is leaving," Adam blamed Eve. "You don't care about the sun. You are always sitting in the shade."

Eve accused Adam, "You always take the sun for granted. I never hear you thank the sun."

While they argued, the sun was sliding from the sky. Down, down, down it went until its red-orange glow faded into the west.

Eve turned to Adam. "Without the sun the plants can't grow! Do something to bring back the sun or else we'll die!" she pleaded.

Adam turned to Eve. "Without the sun, the animals won't find food! Say something to make the sun return, or the world will end!" he cried.

But the sun didn't listen to the first man and the first woman.

"If the sun won't listen, then perhaps God will hear us," said Eve.

"After all," said Adam, "God created the sun."

Adam and Eve sat down beneath the trees in the Garden. As the sky turned to midnight, their eyes began to feel heavy. Together they whispered a prayer. "God, Creator of the Great Light, do not let your world grow dark. Help us bring back the sun. Make morning again."

Adam and Eve looked down at the ground and they noticed dried brown branches and black, smooth rocks. Adam took one rock and Eve another. They began to rub the rocks together. After a long time, sparks lit the branches at their feet. God had taught Adam and Eve how to make fire.

The fire warmed the night chill. But the fire didn't help the plants grow. And it didn't last very long.

Adam and Eve made another fire. It brought light to the midnight sky. But it didn't bring back the sun. The earth became cold and dark.

"I can't take care of it," admitted Adam.

"I can't fix it," sighed Eve.

Once again, they prayed
to God, "God, Creator
of the Great Light, make
morning again." But there
was no answer.

Adam and Eve were afraid
of the dark. It was cold.
The stars in the sky looked
like droplets of ice. Adam and
Eve huddled close together.
They fell asleep waiting for
the world to end.

Then it happened. The eagles awoke in their nests. The sun blushed in the east.

A pink glow wrapped around the mountains and winked behind the clouds. The sky turned purple, then blue.

The rooster crowed and
announced morning at last.
Adam and Eve awoke
to watch the sun paint the
sky with light. The light
wrapped around them
like a robe of gold.

Adam and Eve rubbed the sleep from their eyes. The setting sun was not the end of the world—it was only the coming of the night. They could brighten the night by making fire, by staying together. And now it was the beginning of a new day.

They thanked God for the morning sun and the rooster's call. They thanked God for creating the day and the night, for the light and the dark. And every day, when the wings of the morning lifted the sun in the sky, the first man and the first woman blessed the day.

And every evening when the sun set, they blessed the night as well.

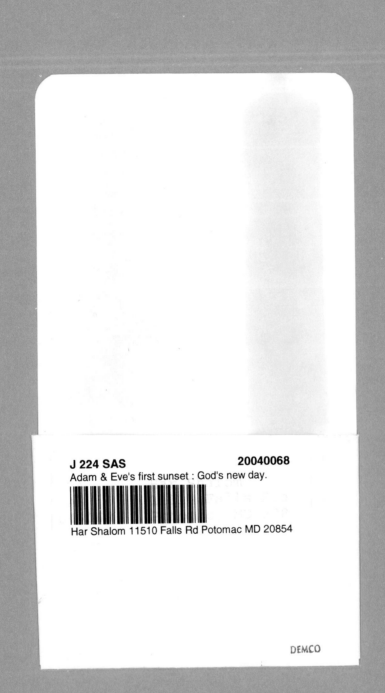